SWEET BOYS LOVE CHRISTMAS

MICALEA SMELTZER

SWEET BOYS LOVE CHRISTMAS

MICALEA SMELTZER

Copyright © 2024 by Micalea Smeltzer

All rights reserved.

No part of this book may be reproduced in any form or by any electronic or mechanical means, including information storage and retrieval systems, without written permission from the author, except for the use of brief quotations in a book review.

Cover Design: Emily Wittig

Edits and Proofread: Beth at VB Edits

Formatting: Micalea Smeltzer

BLURB

Sweet Boys Love Christmas

When my Christmas plans go up in flames the last thing I expect is Luke Covey to sweep in and save the day. Spending the holiday with him and his mom might make this my favorite Christmas I've ever had.
Too bad for me there's one unexpected gift that's going to last long past the holiday season, because ready or not Luke and I are going to be parents.

ONE

Bertie

"Mom? What?" Disbelief hits me like a slap to the face. I have to put her on speaker so I can pace my dorm. "The plan was to go to London as a family for Christmas. What's changed?"

"I told you." She sighs over the line, exasperated. She probably assumes I'm too dense to understand what she's implying. In reality, I get it. That's not the issue. I need to hear her say it instead of beating around the bush. "Your father and I were invited to the Maldives with the Lutzes, so we're going there instead."

"We're?"

"Your father and I."

"But not me."

I knew from the moment I answered the phone that she would break my heart.

My parents aren't horrible people. They've never abused me. I've always had more than I could ask for.

But they are selfish.

All I've ever been to them is an accessory. In the beginning, I was a cute little kid to tote around to their high society functions. "Look at our little Beatrice. Isn't she a doll?"

Except they forgot that babies turn into toddlers, who turn into children, who then become teens and adults. I was mostly raised by a rotation of nannies. It's shocking that I can function like a normal person at all.

"No, sweetie. It's just adults."

With my eyes closed, I clench my teeth. As if I'm not nearly about to graduate from university. I *am* an adult, but to them, I'll always be a pesky child.

"I understand."

I *don't*, but I learned to stop picking fights years ago. It gets me nowhere, and this one would only further prove her point that I'm not mature enough for this *adults-only* trip.

"I knew you would. Talk soon." With that, she ends the call.

Huffing, I toss my phone onto the couch. Then I clutch a throw pillow and bury my face in it while I scream.

I don't hate my parents, but I can't say I like them either.

But I'm tired of being understanding of their whims. When they hurt me like this, they don't even care. That's the worst part.

It doesn't help my mood that I've essentially been alone since my roommate and best friend ditched me months ago. Though it was for a good reason, it left me living on my own, and she's so busy we don't hang out like we used to.

I have other friends, but not ones I trust the way I trust Rosie.

Spending the Christmas holiday by myself on campus may just be the most pathetic thing I could do, but what choice do I have? There's no time to plan a trip, and I don't relish the idea of going alone anyway. I already spend enough time by myself. I don't need to be reminded of how lonely I am by sitting in a hotel room with no company but my own.

Sighing, I push myself up from the couch, then I shrug into my coat. The last place I need to be right now is my empty, silent dorm room.

My frustration mounts as I head across campus to the dining hall.

I hate that I let my mom get me. I hate that I'm disappointed. I should've expected this, and that's on me.

The worst part is that, despite it all, I always believe the best in my parents. Every time, I believe they'll be different, and then I'm inevitably let down.

Fool me once, shame on you. Fool me twice ... or in this case, a hundred times.

A guy leaving the dining hall holds the door for me. "Thanks," I mumble, stepping inside and taking off my mittens. As I shove them into my pocket, I head straight for the dessert station. I deserve a brownie.

With a tray in tow, I pick out one of the brownies, drop a dollop of Cool Whip on top, and finish it off with a few gummy worms. Perfection.

"Rough day?"

I jump at the sound of the voice and whip around, coming face-to-face with my ex.

We've been broken up since the beginning of the school year, which means my rose-colored glasses have been completely removed, and I've settled into the *why the fuck was I so obsessed with this weasel?* stage.

"Hi, Tommy." Hoping we can leave the conversation at that, I move over to the utensil stand and pick up a fork and a small stack of napkins. When he follows, I sigh. "Can I help you?"

"What's with the attitude?" He falls into step behind me as I shuffle through the dining hall. I scan the tables, taking my time looking for one. There are plenty open, but I don't want to sit with him.

"I don't have an attitude."

I'm sad and want to eat my brownie in peace. Is that too much to ask for?

Teeth gritted, I search the open area for someone I might know. Unfortunately, the only person I recognize is Luke Covey, who's seated at a table in a corner, head buried in a book, wearing a pair of wired earbuds that look like they're going to disintegrate if he so much as breathes funny.

"You definitely do." He curls his fingers around my biceps to stop me. "Can we talk?"

Chest tightening, I look from where he's holding me to his face. "Talk? Why?"

He barks out a laugh like *I'm* the crazy one. "About us?"

"Tommy." I fight back the urge to stomp my foot out of frustration. "There is no us."

This is my own fault. I stupidly took him back

multiple times. So naturally, he doesn't believe I was serious when I said it was over for good. It's not the first time he's tried to broach this topic since our last—and final—breakup.

"Come on, babe." He gives my arm a squeeze that's borderline painful. "You don't mean that."

"I very much do." I shrug off his hold.

I should have stayed in my room.

As unease ripples through me at Tommy's proximity, I look back to where I spotted Luke. Now, rather than curled over a book, he's sitting straight, watching us. Concern is etched into the lines of his face.

Sometimes I wish Luke wasn't such a good guy.

He might be a hockey player, but he's not a manwhore like most of our school's team. He's quiet, almost borderline shy, and fucking *hot*.

Unbidden, my thoughts drift to our one and only night together during our freshman year. How his body felt above mine, the gentle way he kissed me.

It was the best sex of my life.

We didn't exchange names or numbers, and afterward, we went on with our lives. It wasn't until this year that I ran into him again. And I keep running into him. We've found ourselves hanging out in the same group of people and have chatted a few times, but he's made it clear that he's interested in something serious. Me?

Though I'm over Tommy, I'm not ready for a relationship.

Across the room, Luke arches a brow and nods at the empty chair across from him.

"I have to go. I'm meeting a friend."

Tommy guffaws. "You're blowing me off?"

"Yes." I step to one side, but he blocks me. "Hey," I snap.

"I want to talk to you." He shuffles in even closer. "You're being ridiculous. You know we're endgame, baby. Please put me out of my misery and—"

A large looming shadow falls over us. Without registering the identity of the interloper, I close my eyes. There's no need to look at him. I'd recognize that clean ocean and slightly salty scent anywhere.

"Are you so dense you can't tell when a woman clearly isn't interested?"

My eyes fly open at the rough timbre of the voice.

Tommy turns, a sneer already on his face. It's laughable, the stark contrast between him and Luke.

Tommy in his preppy gray cardigan and brand-new shoes that were created to look distressed versus Luke in his light blue waffle-knit Henley, oil-stained jeans, and leather boots that look like they've been used and abused for years. Not to mention the striking difference in height. Tommy swears he's six-foot, but five-ten, maybe five-eleven, is more accurate. Luke, on the other hand, is well over six-foot. I'd guess around six-five.

"Our conversation is none of your business." Tommy puts on a tough front, but based on the way his hands are balled at his sides and how big his eyes have gone, he's rattled by the hockey player's presence. Not only is Luke taller, but he's also a hell of a lot more muscular.

"It is my business when a woman is clearly trying to get away from you."

I bite my lip, worry settling into my gut. Luke may play an aggressive sport, but the guy is more of a lover than a fighter.

"What's your problem, man?" Tommy sneers, looking Luke up and down. His lip curls when he notices the tattoos on his forearms. "I'm talking to my girlfriend."

Luke focuses on me, blinking his vivid blue eyes in surprise.

"Ex," I clarify. "Very much ex-girlfriend."

Tommy has the audacity to roll his eyes and let out a huff like a disgruntled toddler. "Babe, be for real—"

"I am." My voice is loud and strong, despite how weak I feel on the inside. All I wanted was to have a little treat and allow myself a moment of pity. Yet I can't even do that because Tommy still thinks he's entitled to my time. "I told you when we broke up that it was for good this time. Move on. I'm begging you."

Tommy, his face turning an unflattering shade of red, knocks the tray out of my hands and straight into Luke's chest before storming out of the dining hall.

The tray clatters to the ground, leaving a glob of Cool Whip on the hockey player's shirt.

"Luke," I breathe, on the verge of tears as a gummy worm falls from his shirt to join the mess on the floor.

"Hey, it's okay." He grasps my shoulders to steady me.

It's only then that I realize I'm swaying on my feet. My heart pangs at the realization that he's comforting me when he's the one covered in my food.

"I'm sorry about that." Sniffling, I frown at his shirt.

He looks down. "Fuck, Bertie, don't worry about my shirt. Washers exist for a reason. Come here. Sit down."

With my lips pressed together, I let him guide me to his table.

"Wait here," he instructs. Then he's shuffling back to the tray and plate on the floor.

I want to burst into tears when he kneels and helps one of the dining hall workers clean up the mess, despite her protests. Tommy would never do such a thing. He'd deem such a task beneath him. Luke is so different from the guys I grew up around. I guess that's what draws me to him. He's *real*.

Once the mess is gone, he doesn't return right away. A wave of disappointment hits me as he walks away from me, but when he gets in line, I really do have to fight back tears.

Only a minute later, he approaches the table and sets a plate in front of me. The replacement brownie is covered in Cool Whip and gummy worms, just like my original treat. Beside the plate is a fresh spoon and napkins.

Luke Covey is too good for this world, and he's definitely too damn good for me.

"Don't cry." He picks his backpack up off the floor and sets it on a chair, then rifles through the contents. "I won't be able to stand it if you cry."

"Why are you so nice to me?" I pick up the spoon and scoop a bit of the brownie and Cool Whip in one bite.

What kind of guy bothers to come to the aid of a girl who's blown him off more than once?

He arches a brow, pulling a clean shirt from his bag. "Why *wouldn't* I be nice to you?"

Lips parted, I blink up at him. "Because I turned you down?"

Rather than respond, he shrugs out of his stained shirt, completely bare-chested in the dining hall, showing off olive-toned skin peppered with ink. I greedily take it in, noting the several pieces that didn't exist when we hooked up years ago.

He pulls the clean shirt on, and I nearly whimper in

protest as the gorgeous view is covered up. But, somehow, Luke in a plain white tee is almost more lethal.

He's the complete opposite of Tommy. Close-cropped dark hair and stubbled jaw to Tommy's slicked-back sandy brown hair and clean-shaven face. His face is sharp, angular, whereas Tommy is almost baby-faced.

Luke settles in the seat across from me. "You think that because you said no when I asked you on a date, I wouldn't stand up for you when a guy is clearly being a dick? If that's the kind of guy you think I am, then you don't know me at all."

My stomach sinks. "I ... that's not what I meant."

He taps his fingers on top of the table. "Then what did you mean?"

"I don't know," I answer softly, gaze lowered to the tray in front of me. "I guess I'm not used to guys like you."

Hurt flashes across his face. Clearly, he's misinterpreted my words. "Guys like me. Got it."

I clear my throat and force myself to hold eye contact. "I meant that you're a good guy, and the guys I'm used to..."

"Aren't? Who are you hanging out with?" His lips twitch with a barely there smile.

"I mean"—I wiggle my fingers, indicating what just

happened—"look at how my ex acted. You didn't even get mad when you ended up covered in my food."

Head tilted, he frowns. "Why would I get mad about that?"

My shoulders crawl up to my ears. "A lot of guys would."

Luke shakes his head, swiping a half-full bottle of water from the table. He uncaps it and takes a sip. "You need to hang out with better people."

I don't know what makes me say it, but the words tumble out. "Are you implying I should hang out with you?"

"No, actually."

I wince at the way his words sting.

"I've made it clear I'm interested in you," he says, his tone gentle. "I like you. A lot. I don't want to just be your friend."

My chest tightens at the admission. I have to say, I respect the guy for being honest.

"Right." I lower my head and grasp the edges of my tray. "I'll go to a different table."

He puts his hand on the tray with enough pressure that I can't move it. "Stay. Eat your treat and tell me what happened."

"What happened?" I ask stupidly.

He sits back, rubbing a hand over his stubbled jaw.

His blue eyes are an endless ocean I could drown in. The long dark lashes only make them more gorgeous. How unfair. My lashes are almost white. I have to coat them with mascara even if I'm not wearing any other makeup.

"You were sad when you came in. Tell me about it."

He noticed my mood when I came in? My breath hitches at the idea. I should keep my mouth shut, but I find the words tumbling out anyway. "It was my mom. I was supposed to go to London with my parents over Christmas, but they got invited to the Maldives with friends, so they canceled on me, and I'll just be here." I shrug, scooping a gummy worm off my plate. "I know what you're thinking. *Oh, poor little rich girl can't go to London.* Really, though, I *could* go by myself. But I just..." I bite down on the gummy worm, tear the chunk off a little too violently, and chew it up. "I guess I'm tired of having to work for my parents' affection. I'm tired of never truly getting it. I want them to see me as a person, not an accessory."

The sympathy in Luke's eyes has me wanting to crawl under the table and dig my way out of this building.

"I wasn't thinking that about you," he says, lacing his fingers on the table. "Don't assume you know what I think. But I am sorry your parents make you feel that way."

"Sorry, I just..." I gesture between us.

"I may be a scholarship student, but I don't walk around here judging all of you who aren't. Okay," he drawls, "maybe sometimes." He winks in a way that makes my stomach stir. "What are you doing for the holiday instead?"

Sighing, I rest my chin in my hand. "I'll be here. I don't see the point in doing something now. It would only remind me of how alone I really am."

Sitting taller, he angles in. "You won't be alone."

"Uh, yeah, I will be."

He cocks his head to the side. "I'll be around. We can hang out," he says. "As friends."

"You're not going back home?"

He shakes his head. "I'm from here."

"Oh." I study him, processing the suggestion. "Yeah, we can hang out."

"Cool." He tries to play it off, but he can't hide the twitch of his lips that tells me he's pleased with my answer. He clears his throat, the tips of his ears turning slightly red. It's endearing and surprising that this insanely good-looking man has this shyness about him. "I just want you to know that I respect that you're not ready to date. I don't want to push you into anything. I just ... I do like spending time with you."

Smiling back, I pat his hand. "I like spending time with you, too."

A part of me wishes I wasn't so hell-bent on being independent after being with Tommy for so long, especially when said independence consists of spending most of my free time alone in my dorm eating way too much popcorn and binging all my favorite shows. It's clear that Luke genuinely likes me, and he's a good guy. But I made a promise to myself, and I'll continue to uphold it.

I polish off the last of my dessert, wipe my face, and drop my napkin onto my plate. "Thanks again. I guess I'll see you around."

With a nod, he opens his book back up. "I'm sure you will." When I stand and turn to leave, he tacks on, "Bye, Bertie."

The tenderness in his voice is soothing. I hesitate for a moment, wondering if I should take it all back—tell him I was wrong when I said I didn't want something serious. But I shake my head, pick up my tray, and take off.

Two

L uke

"Hey, Mama." I press a quick kiss to my mom's cheek.

Her shoulders are stooped, and her face is drawn in exhaustion, but she's still at the stove making dinner.

Even though I want to shower and crawl into bed after a brutal practice, I take the wooden spoon from her and shoo her over to a chair. "I'll take over with this."

"Thanks, Lukie."

Grunting, I peer at her over my shoulder. My mom is

the only person on the planet I'll let get away with calling me that.

At the table, she pulls off her sneakers and rubs at the bottoms of her feet.

The sight of her after a long day at work always makes me second-guess not entering the NHL draft last summer. With the kind of money I'd be making, I could've easily retired her. But she was resolute in her argument that I finish my degree first. My agent wasn't happy when I delayed another year, and he's been on my ass more than ever since then, making sure I'm at the top of my game. In my eyes, another year of experience at the college level will only help me. But his argument is that teams are starting to veer toward younger players—ones they can mold into what they need, ones who don't have the additional four years of habits to break.

I shove that worry aside quickly. Otherwise I'll induce an anxiety attack.

I don't care about being filthy rich, but I do care about taking care of my mom.

My dad left when I was a baby, and though he popped in and out sporadically over the years, my mom raised me all on her own. All I want now is to help her. The first thing I'll do is pay off this house. Then I'll take care of her bills so she can slow down and appreciate life.

When the Hamburger Helper—a staple in our household—is done, I pick up one plate she's already set out and scoop a helping onto it. Fork in hand, I set her dinner in front of her. Then I head for the hall.

"Luke, you should eat," she calls after me.

Without looking back, I wave a dismissive hand. "I want to shower."

The instant I'm locked in the bathroom, I grip the counter and take several deep breaths. I *should* eat. With the number of calories I burn, I need it. But after today's encounter, my brain is muddled and spinning in circles. If I eat now, I'll probably throw it up.

The last thing I should be thinking about is Bertie Carthwright, a girl a billion light-years out of my league for so many reasons, but especially because she's practically old-money American royalty. Her family is most well-known for their Carthwright Chocolate Bar. But the company they've owned for generations has branched out far beyond the candy-making industry. I know because I googled it after I met her during freshman year. After reading article after article, I spiraled even worse than I am now.

I turn the shower on, and while the water heats, I yank my shirt off and drop it into the laundry basket.

Sometimes I wish I could be more like the guys on my team who hook up regularly and don't want to be tied down. Sure, I've had one-night stands here and there—

Bertie was one, after all—but I *want* a girlfriend. And I want more than just sex. I want a deep connection. To eat dinners with my girl. Cuddle on the couch. Talk about the mundane shit.

If the guys knew, they'd roast me for the rest of my life.

I worry about making it into the NHL and only attracting women who want me for my money. I want someone to love *me*, not what might be in my bank account.

When the water is warm, I strip out of my jeans and briefs, then step inside. It's routine now, to duck as I do, since I'm inches taller than the height of the shower nozzle. I showered after practice, but there's no way I can relax until I do it again when I get home.

I was diagnosed with OCD in high school. It doesn't always manifest in ways the world thinks it does. For me, it's things like having to shower when I get home from practice, even if my hair is still damp from my post-practice shower. It was my high school hockey coach who first suspected something. I'm not even sure what clued him in, but since he has OCD, too, it probably made it easier for him to put two and two together. He spoke with my mom and me about it, and while I know it was an added stress for her, she got me to the right doctors.

My compulsions aren't as bad as they used to be—

back then, there were days they would downright consume me—but they're still there, and they get worse if I'm stressed.

After the shower, I change into a pair of sweatpants and a hoodie. Then I pad into my room, unsurprised to find a plate of dinner covered in foil waiting for me.

My chest tightens. Dammit. I hate that my mom worries so much about me.

She believes it's her job to worry about me and not the other way around, but all I want is to ease her stress. Her hovering doesn't bother me in the way she probably thinks it does. It doesn't annoy me, but it does make me feel guilty. It's hard not to hate that even after raising me on her own for eighteen years, she still feels the need to look out for me.

Sitting on the edge of my bed, I pick up the plate. I take a few bites, then set it down again. It's all I can manage.

After I've put my plate in the fridge, thankfully avoiding my mom and her concern, I lock myself in my room and reply to the group text with my team. Then, lying back on the bed, I scroll through my text messages until I come across Bertie.

After she told me she wasn't interested in a relationship, and I told her I wasn't interested in just being a hookup, it didn't feel right to text her, even though I genuinely like her as a person, so I stopped. I worried she might think I was hoping to get her to change her mind and date me.

She said no, and I respect that.

But I am worried about her after running into her in the dining hall today. The moment she came in, she was on my radar. I'm hyperaware of that girl. It's like the air shifts when she's around me and I *know* she's there. All it took was a single look to know she was upset. Then her douchebag ex had to go and make things worse.

With a sigh, I grab my book off the table beside my bed. Reading is one of the things that helps my OCD most. Though it might've become a bit of a compulsion, too. Often, I lose myself in working to see how quickly I can finish a book or in considering how many I can read in a week, a month, a year.

Right now, though, it isn't enough to distract me from my phone, which continues to taunt me from beside me on the bed. Finally, when I can't take it anymore, I set the book down and text her.

> Me: Hey, I just wanted to check in and make sure you're okay.

I hold my breath, waiting for a response. A minute passes. Two. Each time the screen darkens, I swipe to wake it again.

Finally, those little bubbles that tell me she's replying appear.

> Bertie: Define okay.

I'm considering how to respond when another message pops up.

> Bertie: If okay means eating an entire bag of Doritos while watching One Tree Hill, then I'm doing fan-fucking-tastic.

Heart aching for her, I go with a simple response.

> Me: That bad, huh?

Those dots appear, disappear, and appear again.

> Bertie: I'm just being whiny. I should've expected them to ditch me.

I hold my phone, thumbs positioned over the display, contemplating how best to word what I say. I don't want to make her feel even shittier than she already does.

Saying *you deserve better parents* or *sounds like they fucking suck* won't help.

> Me: Maybe it's a sign that better things are coming to you for the break.

> Bertie: Like what? A deal on delivery pizza and my vibrator magically possessing the ability to never need a charge?

> Bertie: I'm REALLY sorry for the vibrator comment. I might've gotten into the whine. Oops.

> Bertie: Wien

> Bertie: WINE

I'm grinning at my phone like a lunatic. She's fucking adorable.

> Me: I am sorry they ditched you. It was shitty of them.

> Bertie: What can I say, they're shitty parents.

I read over her message a few times, a lump in my throat, before I respond.

> Me: Sometimes people who become parents are kind of clueless about how to do the job. There isn't a handbook.

> Bertie: If I ever become a mom, I don't want to be like mine. Is that horrible of me?

> Me: Based on what your mom sounds like, not at all.

> Bertie: I want to be there for my kid. Stick their scribbled drawings on the fridge and cry when they go to their first day of school and pack lunches and go to school plays and … I just want to be THERE, ya know?

I do. And I know how lucky I am to have a parent who has always been there for me, despite how hard she works. Even now, she never misses a home hockey game. It wasn't cheap, keeping me outfitted in hockey gear as I grew up. She had to get a lot of my stuff secondhand. Honestly, I don't think I'll ever know how much she sacrificed so that I didn't have to go without.

> Me: Yeah, I know what you mean.

> Bertie: Now that you know how shitty my family is, tell me about yours.

Smiling at my phone, I roll onto my side. I'm not even sure why I'm smiling like a fucking goober except that I'm talking to Bertie. Something about this girl makes me downright giddy.

> Me: My dad has never really been in the picture. He's popped up from time to time over the years, but I've never viewed him as a fatherly figure. He gives off more of a fun uncle vibe, I guess. My mom is amazing, though. She got pregnant at eighteen and raised me on her own when her family wrote her off. She's my best friend.

> Bertie: My first instinct is to tell you that it's incredibly cheesy that your mom is your best friend, but honestly, I'm jealous. You're lucky to have her.

> Me: I know it. Who did you have, B?

Even though she's not here with me, I swear I can hear her sigh.

> Bertie: I had myself and my dolls, and once in a while, I had a good nanny.

Bertie's family might have more money than I can comprehend, but right about now, it's hard not to feel like I'm the privileged one. Money is great and all, but being genuinely loved and cared for is better.

> Me: That's ... kind of sad.

> Bertie: It's totally pathetic, but you asked, and it's the truth.

> Bertie: Sometimes I think if I didn't call my parents, they'd forget about me entirely.

> Me: I'm sure that's not true.

Or maybe it is. But I don't want to agree with her. She's clearly already wallowing in her feelings. There's no use making it worse.

> Bertie: It totally is, but it's okay.

> Bertie: Actually, it's not okay, but it is what it is. When I have kids, I'll make sure they know how special and loved they are.

My heart breaks thinking about little Bertie just wanting love and affection from her parents and receiving none of it. It's probably a miracle she turned out to be so sweet and kind.

> Me: I'm sure you'll be a good mom one day.

> Bertie: Thanks. I'm going to go now. You're making me cry.

Fuck. My heart cracks right down the middle at the thought.

> Me: I didn't mean to.

> Bertie: Oh, I know. I always cry when I've had too much to drink. I'll be better in the morning. Promise.

> Me: Is it okay if I check in with you tomorrow?

It takes several minutes for her reply to come in. While I wait, anxiety threading through me, I worry I've pushed her too far. My mind has started to spiral inside my head when a message finally comes through a few minutes later.

> Bertie: Sorry, I think I dozed off for a second there. But yes, that's fine.

> Me: Cool. Go to bed.

> Bertie: I will and thanks for talking to me. I do feel better.

> Me: Anytime.

THREE

Bertie

SNOW FLURRIES CHASE ME AROUND CAMPUS. Though it's cold, I can't help but relish in the elation that's hit me today. I'm tempted to stick my tongue out and spin in a circle to see if I can catch a flake. That's how happy I am to have finals behind me and freedom ahead. One more semester down and only one to go until graduation.

I'm still annoyed with my parents, but there's nothing I can do about it now. I've hyped myself up for a

Christmas alone. I decorated my dorm with a small tree I picked up at Target, created a plan for a movie marathon, and ordered Christmas-themed pajamas galore.

All I can do is make the best of it. I even ordered a few presents for myself and had them gift-wrapped so I can open them on Christmas. Sure, I know what's inside each one, but chances are high my mom will forget to send me anything.

The holiday isn't about gifts, of course, but the reminder that my parents forget my existence stings. This way, I'll at least have a few new items of clothing and handbags to keep me company.

Although, now that I think about it, that might only make me feel more alone than I already am.

With my thoughts racing and my stomach turning, I let myself into the coffee shop on campus. Once I place my order for a peppermint mocha, I wait off to the side and send a text to Rosie, though I don't expect a response any time soon. She's busy these days.

I have other friends on campus, but they've all headed home for the holidays. Rosie, on the other hand, lives close by and is celebrating Christmas here with her family.

When my order is up, I grab it and head back out into the chilly December weather.

Now that finals are done and I won't have studying to

occupy my time, I'm not sure what to do with myself. It's been way too long since I've been to the gym, and that would distract me, but the idea of running on the treadmill or lifting weights doesn't sound appealing at the moment.

I could go to the movies. Or shopping. I think there's some sort of light festival happening in a nearby town.

Maybe I should do that tonight.

So absorbed in my thoughts, I run straight into a person—luckily without spilling my coffee. As I bounce off his hard chest, I'm already spewing apologies.

"I'm so sorry. I wasn't—"

Luke takes one of his earbuds out and smiles in a way that makes his eyes crinkle at the corners.

My stomach dips in response. I never got butterflies like this with Tommy. Maybe that's why Luke scares me so much. Because if I gave him a chance and things didn't work out, I'd never recover.

"Hey, are you okay?" he asks.

"Fine," I answer a little too curtly. With a breath in, I will myself to relax and give him a smile. "Just finished my last final and wanted coffee." I hold up my cup.

We've been texting here and there since that day at the dining hall. Nothing serious, though.

"Where are you headed?" he asks, spinning the

earbud back and forth between his thumb and index finger.

"I guess back to my dorm. I don't really have anywhere else to be."

With a nod, he adjusts his beanie. "Listen, I don't want to sound too forward, and I don't want you to think I'm only offering this because I like you." His cheeks pinken, and not because of the chill in the air. "But I've been thinking about you being alone for Christmas and..." He sighs, tugging the beanie off entirely to rub his fingers over his closely cropped hair. "My mom always cooks a meal on Christmas Eve. It's just us two and it's a lot of food. You should come over. If you want. She'd love to have someone else to feed and shower with Christmas spirit."

My heart thumps heavily in my chest as I mull over the idea. Christmas is still about two weeks away. "Can I think about it and get back to you?"

He gives me a half smile. "Sure. See you." He sticks his earbud back in and walks away.

It's cold. I should be scurrying away, eager to get inside and warm up, but I watch until he disappears into one of the buildings before I make my way back to my dorm.

Inside, I set the paper cup down and plug in the lights

I wrapped around the small Christmas tree. Instantly, the warm twinkling light makes the space feel homier.

Sipping my coffee, I shuffle to the fridge in search of leftovers.

I locate a bowl of pasta I made a few nights ago. It passes the sniff test, so I stick it in the microwave to start the warming process while I hop into the shower.

Once I've dried off, I pull on my coziest flannel pajamas and fuzzy socks, probably looking ridiculous, but I'm not trying to impress anyone.

I give my pasta a quick stir, stick it in the microwave for another thirty seconds, then bring it over to the couch and cue up a Christmas movie. I've already watched all my favorites this holiday season, so I'm expanding my horizons and trying a few I've never seen.

Before I can hit play, I'm overwhelmed with the urge to text Luke. Why, I couldn't say. Maybe because I ran into him or maybe because I'm lonely. Either way, I don't give myself time to second-guess it.

> Me: Please feel free to say no, but would you want to come over and watch Christmas movies with me?

Nerves skitter through me as I wait for his reply. I don't want to sound too needy or desperate.

I've just about convinced myself to start the movie and forget about it when his reply comes through.

> Luke: I'd like that. Should I bring food?

> Me: Only if you're hungry. I'm eating leftovers.

> Luke: Cool. Dessert?

> Me: I'll never say no to dessert.

> Luke: Any preference?

> Me: CHOCOLATE.

> Me: Also anything with peanut butter.

> Luke: Got it. See you soon.

I send him the information he needs to get inside my dorm building, then sit back and exhale. Only then does the realization that Luke is coming *here* wash over me. Which, honestly, I should've thought about *before* I asked him.

My bra is draped over the chair.

There's a shoe halfway under the TV console.

My laptop has streaks of Hershey's chocolate smeared on it from when I was stuffing my face while studying, but it looks suspiciously like something else.

"Shit."

I stick my mostly uneaten leftovers back in the fridge, then rush around picking up the space.

I'm normally a tidy person, but after I discovered my parents were ditching me for Christmas, I might've wallowed a bit. Or a lot.

Once I've picked up the clutter, I wipe down counters, clean up the smear of toothpaste from the sink in case he has to use the bathroom, and stuff my tampons in the cabinet.

As I straighten and close the cabinet door, I catch sight of myself in the mirror, and a curse springs out of me.

I'm a mess. My blond hair is piled on top of my head, and my pajamas are far from cute. I look nowhere near desirable.

Not that I want him to see me as such.

We're just two platonic friends hanging out.

So, with a heavy exhale, I decide to keep the pajamas. But I have to do something about my hair. I let it down and carefully brush out the knots. How it got so tangled in such a short amount of time is beyond me. Once my hair is smooth, I spritz a little perfume on, worried that I stink and just can't tell.

I've just put it away when there's a knock at my door.

Smoothing my hands down the front of my pajamas, I

give myself five seconds to catch my breath before I turn the knob and greet my visitor.

Luke takes up the entire doorway. He's so big in the narrow hallway outside my dorm. Larger than life.

"Hey." His lips quirk up on one side. "I went ahead and got you a veggie pizza just in case."

He holds up the two boxes, breaking me out of my trance.

"Thanks." I step aside to let him in. "I ended up not eating my leftovers, so this is great."

His dark brows furrow as he sets the pizza on the counter. "Why didn't you eat?"

"I needed to clean up. This place was a mess."

A gruff laugh escapes him. "You didn't need to clean up for me." He looks around my dorm, taking in the kitchenette and living area with the two bedrooms branching off and a bathroom between. "I forget how nice these rooms are. It's like an apartment."

I cross my arms over my chest, but immediately drop them again when I realize I'm not wearing a bra. "You don't live on campus?"

He shakes his head. "I'm a local, remember? I live with my mom." His cheeks flame a little at that, like he's embarrassed about his living situation. "I think that's part of the reason I got the scholarship here. Help out a local kid or whatever."

"I'm pretty sure it's your hockey talent that got you in." The instant the words are out, I want to slap myself. Now I'm the one whose cheeks are heating.

He grins, making a dimple I've never noticed pop. This man was already lethal, but throw in a dimple, and I'm not sure I stand any chance.

"Checking out my stats, B?"

Nobody in my life calls me B except him, and I don't correct him. For some ridiculous reason, I like it.

"I was looking at the whole team."

His eyes glimmer with amusement. "I'm sure you were."

"You know you're a good player," I mutter, standing on my tiptoes to grab plates from the cabinet. "You don't need me to tell you that."

"No." He steps up behind me and presses a hand against my waist. "But I do like to hear it." His body is warm behind mine. "Let me get those."

Our fingers graze as we reach for the plates at the same time, and sparks zip up my arm like I've been electrocuted.

"Sorry," I mutter, quickly pulling my hand against my chest and dropping down so my feet are flat on the floor.

"No, I'm sorry," he says, setting the plates on the counter and putting a foot of space between us.

We silently load our plates, then sit on the couch with matching cans of Diet Coke.

"What movie do you want to watch?" he asks, shifting back and widening his long legs.

The couch is small, closer to love seat size, yet he miraculously manages to leave inches of space between us.

I both hate and love that space.

Love it, because he's respecting my wishes.

Hate it, because dammit, I really want him to breach that line.

"I planned to watch something I never have before, but honestly"—I pick up the remote from the coffee table—"I'm not feeling it. I think I'm in the mood for *Home Alone*. Is that good with you?"

"Absolutely. It's a masterpiece." He takes a bite of pizza and groans, his eyes closing for a moment. "Still can't figure out how you forget your kid at home." He turns slowly in my direction, blinking. "Please tell me your parents never forgot you at home."

"Probably a time or two," I answer honestly. "But I always had nannies, so their asses were covered."

He lowers his head and gives it a shake. "That's terrible."

"Yeah, I know. I think..." I twist my lips back and

forth, considering whether I want to voice this out loud. "I don't think they wanted kids, but my grandparents wanted the legacy to be carried on, so ta-da, there's me. Except I'm not a man, and even if my future spouse would take my last name, I don't think I would want them to. It feels more like a curse than a blessing."

"What's it like?"

"What's what like?" I scroll through my movies, looking for *Home Alone* in the recently watched category.

"Being a Carthwright."

A heavy sigh filters out of me. "In one word? Exhausting."

He's still watching me, as if that isn't enough of an answer.

"Don't get me wrong. It comes with a lot of privileges," I say, focused on the plate of pizza in my lap. "Shopping sprees, the fanciest restaurants, and opportunities galore. But it also comes with a lot of pressure. When people know who you are, they're always watching and inevitably waiting for you to fuck up. The pressure to be perfect is intense. I went to the best private school and had the smartest tutors and anything I could want, but…"

"But?" He probes, ducking a little closer.

"But I was lonely." I shrug, pressing the button on the remote to start the movie. "As a little kid, I wished more than once that I had a different family. I was spoiled, sure. Any toy I showed even mild interest in appeared in my room, but that wasn't what I wanted. I just ... wanted my mom and dad."

He's quiet for a moment, a slice of pizza hanging limply in his hand. "I'm sorry it was like that for you."

I shrug, lips pressed together. "At least I turned out okay."

With the movie playing, conversation ceases, and we dig into our dinner in earnest. When we've both had our fill, Luke rinses the plates in the sink. My core clenches at the sight of him stooped over the sink scrubbing. Am I crazy for not pursuing a relationship with him? He's gorgeous, and he's a talented hockey player. Not to mention he's smart and kind.

No. I'm not crazy. I just need more time. I was with Tommy for so long, and I've forgotten what it's like to be an individual.

I don't *like* being alone, but it's important for my growth.

Luke returns to the couch, and when I tug the throw blanket off the back and spread it out, he happily accepts one half of it, though he doesn't speak. I like that he doesn't push conversation. He's just ... there. And it's comfortable. The silence between us.

I didn't have that with Tommy.

When things got quiet, I always felt like I needed to chatter to avoid the awkwardness that would settle in.

"Do you want to watch another movie?" I ask when *Home Alone* finishes. "Do you need to be somewhere?"

He shakes his head. "I have time."

With a small smile, I pass him the remote. "You pick this time."

His hand brushes mine as he takes it, and another spark courses up my arm.

"You sure?"

"Yeah."

With a nod, he browses through my movies, and after a moment, he settles on *Elf*, then sets the remote on the arm of the couch.

"Solid choice." I adjust my legs since my left foot is beginning to go numb.

"It's a classic." He crosses his arms over his chest, eyes focused on the screen.

As the movie starts, I can't help but stare at him.

Carved cheekbones, with the perfect amount of stubble. Brows I can't help but be envious of—thick and full and perfectly arched, whereas I have to draw mine in or they're practically non-existent. Perfectly full lips.

"I can feel you staring at me."

I let out a sound that can only be described as a yip. "Sorry."

My face goes so hot I have little doubt that it's tomato red.

"It's okay. Look your fill." He keeps his eyes on the TV, but his lips quirk.

I drop my gaze to the blanket in my lap, tugging on a loose strand.

He shifts, causing the couch to creak under his weight. "Don't be embarrassed."

I startle when his finger is suddenly on my chin, forcing my gaze up, and a shiver works its way down my spine.

"We're mature enough to acknowledge that we're attracted to each other. We've both said our piece, and that's that, but attraction doesn't just go away. I'd like to be friends, though."

It's on the tip of my tongue to tell him that I don't think we can be friends. It's not normal to be this attracted to a person one has a platonic relationship with. But I swallow the words down. I'd rather have Luke in this limited capacity than not at all. That's a scary thought, but I can't deny it. My circle is next to nonexistent since I ended things with Tommy. I have Rosie, because she was my friend first. While I have other "friends," the vast majority took Tommy's side when we split. Why there even has to be sides is beyond me, but people are weird. I guess it's better to know now who actually likes me and who just tolerated me because of my boyfriend.

"What are you thinking about over there?" he asks, pausing the movie. He drapes his arm over the back of the couch, his fingers close enough to graze my shoulder if he wanted.

"You don't want to know."

He purses his lips, cocking a brow.

Huffing, I let my shoulders sink. "Tommy."

His nose crinkles like he smells something spoiled. "You're right. I don't want to know."

"I was thinking about how the people in our friend group were actually his friends, and now I'm alone. I have Rosie, of course, and she's great, but she has *a lot* going on right now."

Luke laughs. "I'd say. She married Daire. That's all I need to know."

"Yeah." Head lowered, I pick at the thread on the blanket again. Their marriage is a farce. They tied the knot so Daire can get shared custody of his son. But that obviously isn't public knowledge, so I keep my mouth shut on that front. "I know I'm not missing out on anything, because clearly those people didn't care about me, but I guess with the whole thing with my parents, I'm feeling extra sensitive and lonely."

My stomach twists as I force my gaze up. I can't believe I admitted that to Luke Covey, of all people.

Luke's lips turn down. "I don't like the thought of you being lonely."

I shrug. "I'll be fine. I'll graduate and move on with my life."

His frown deepens. The look causes unease to wash through me. I hate that I'm the one who put it there.

"Don't worry about me," I say, forcing myself to sit straighter. "I'm good. Promise."

He hums, clearly not buying what I'm selling. "Well, if you're ever not good and want to hang out, let me know."

"I did ask you to come over tonight," I remind him.

That pulls a genuine smile from him. "You did." With that, he turns back to the movie.

We're quiet, focused on Buddy the Elf and his shenanigans for a long while. It's a relief, this reprieve from talking about my miserable existence.

I blink several times, my eyelids heavy, and the next thing I know, I'm sinking into my plush mattress.

"What's happening?" I mutter, half asleep.

A quiet shush comes from the darkness. "You fell asleep. I'm tucking you into bed, and then I'm going to head out."

"Oh." I pout at Luke's blurry silhouette. "I didn't snore, did I?"

"No." His chuckle is deep and rumbly, sweeping over me like a physical caress. "But you did drool."

"Oh, God." I wipe at my mouth.

With his fingers wrapped around my wrist gently, he tugs my hand away. "I think you got most of it on my shirt."

Stomach sinking, I cover my face. "*No.*" I draw out the word. "That's so embarrassing. I'm sorry. You're never going to want to see me again."

He pulls the covers up to my shoulders. If I weren't wishing I could crawl into a hole and die, I would think it's cute.

"I could never not want to see you." The confession is barely audible.

As tears prick at the backs of my eyes, I swallow thickly, fighting back emotion.

"Think about spending Christmas Eve with me and my mom, okay? I think you'd like her."

My heart pangs at the thought. "She raised you. I'm sure she's great."

"She really is." He straightens and clears his throat. "Sleep tight." Then he's turning and shuffling to the door.

"Luke?" I rasp.

Silently, he turns around.

"Text me when you get home, okay?"

He nods. "I will."

It takes concerted effort, but I manage to stay awake until his text comes through. Once my phone is on my nightstand and I close my eyes, I drift off quickly.

I'm treading in dangerous water.

It wouldn't take much for me to fall for this man.

FOUR

Luke

I WASN'T EXPECTING TO SPEND ONE OF MY precious winter break days filling in at the diner, working alongside my mom, but here we are. I won't complain about a little extra cash, though. When she mentioned that they'd be short-staffed today, there was no hiding how frazzled she was, so I volunteered to fill in. I've known Harry, the owner, practically all my life, so over the years, I've taken a shift here or there.

Another thing I wasn't expecting today? To see Bertie walk into the diner.

She sports a light pink beanie with some sort of fluffy thing on top that bobs as she walks. Her cheeks are a deeper shade of pink from the chilly temperature, and her coat—yet another shade of pink—is thick and fluffy.

She stands just inside the door, scanning the dining room for a moment, before she heads toward an empty booth in my mom's section.

Mom immediately steps that way, ready to greet her, but I stop her with a hand on her wrist. "I've got this one."

"Oh?" She arches a brow and studies me.

"It's not like that," I warn her, before she can create an elaborate narrative in her head filled with marriage and babies for me and the pretty blonde.

Bertie has her eyes on the menu, so she doesn't notice me approach.

"Are you stalking me?"

She jumps, and when she finds me standing with a pad at the ready, her eyes light in surprise. "What? No. I didn't know you worked here. I ..." She surveys me, then glances around the diner. "Wow, it really does seem like I'm stalking you. I can go."

She starts to slide out of the booth, but I shake my

head and keep my position close to the table so she can't escape.

"I'm just messing with you, B. And no, technically, I don't work here, but they're short-staffed and needed the help. What can I get you to drink?"

"Diet Coke, please."

"You got it." I tap my pen against the pad. "Do you need another minute with the menu?"

She nods, so I give her a smile and leave her to peruse the options while I get her drink.

She watches me as I walk away. Her attention is palpable, even if I can't see her. As I'm scooping ice into a red plastic cup, my mom comes up beside me.

"She's pretty," she singsongs, bumping her elbow playfully into my arm, making the ice clack against the cup.

"She is," I agree. "But again, it's not like that."

She laughs. "Then why is she looking at you like she wants to take a bite?"

Heat creeps up my neck and cheeks as I fill the cup with Diet Coke.

Mom giggles beside me. "Do you like her, Lukie? Ask her out."

If only the floor would open up and swallow me whole right about now.

I was a shy kid, and while I've certainly grown out of

it a bit, I do still have my moments, like this one, where it feels my skin is on fire and the desperation to flee is strong.

"I have asked her out," I whisper. "She doesn't want to date right now. She ended a serious relationship not too long ago."

She frowns. "But you like her."

"Yes," I confirm, even though I'm not sure it was a question.

"And she looks like she's interested in you," she muses.

"Mom," I beg. "Please, stay out of it. We're friends."

She puts her hands up in surrender. "Okay. I'll keep quiet."

Even though I don't want to. Those words hang between us, but I ignore them and head back over to Bertie's table.

"Did you decide yet?"

Nodding, she sticks the menu back in the holder at the other end of the table. "I'll take a cheeseburger—no tomato—and fries, please."

"You got it."

I turn to leave so I can enter her order into the system, but her soft "hey, Luke?" has me swinging back around to face her.

"Thank you again," she says, peering up at me

through her lashes. "For hanging out with me the other day."

"Bertie, you've got to stop thanking me for stuff like that. We're friends. Friends hang out."

"Right." She tucks a piece of hair behind her ear, lowering her head. "Friends."

The sadness in her tone puzzles me. She's the one who doesn't want to be more than that.

She doesn't stop me this time as I turn and walk away to put the order in.

"We're slowing down a bit," my mom says after Bertie's order is in the system and I've refilled another patron's water. "Why don't you take a break and sit with your friend?"

"Mom," I groan at her meddling.

"What?" She blinks innocently. "She looks lonely."

I look back in Bertie's direction. Dammit. I can't deny that she's right. She *does* look lonely, and from what she said the other night, there's a good chance she is.

"Fine," I agree. "But I'm telling her you're meddling."

She laughs as she saunters to one of her tables. "Tell her whatever you want, sweetie."

Grumbling, I put in a discounted order for myself. Now that I'm thinking about a break, I'm ravenous. I've been here since the breakfast rush. How my mom does this day in and day out baffles me. It'll be the best day of my life when I can afford to retire her.

While I wait for our orders, I take care of my tables, ensuring everyone has what they need, and when our meals are up, I carry them both over to Bertie's table.

She frowns in confusion as I slide in across from her.

"Just so you know"—I point at my plate—"this wasn't my idea. My mom is meddling."

Brow furrowed, she peers around the diner. "Your mom is here?"

"Yeah, she works here."

"Ah." She nods. "Now I see why you're here working."

I shrug. "They needed the help."

She points a fry at me. "But you really did it for your mom, didn't you?"

As I unroll my silverware from my napkin, I duck my head and mutter a "yes."

She shakes her head, a smile curling her lips. "You're making it really hard, you know?" A flush stains her creamy skin as soon as the words are out, but she doesn't look away.

I press my lips together, my heart rate picking up a little. "What am I making hard?"

The blush deepens. "Not to change my mind about the whole dating thing." She stuffs a fry into her mouth like it'll keep any more words at bay.

I chuckle, amused. "I promise you, I'm not expecting you to change your mind."

"No, I know that," she says quickly, like she's worried she's offended me. "I only meant ... you're a really great guy, and it's obviously not an act. I can't see you ever being one of those guys who tries to do that. A true good guy doesn't feel the need and—"

"Take a breath." I angle over the table and make sure she's looking at me. "Just so you know, it's okay to have feelings for someone and not act on them. You know how I feel about you, and I won't pressure you for more. I don't want you to think that I'm hanging out with you to try to get you to change your mind either."

"I know, I know," she chants, hiding her mouth behind her hand while she chews. "I just meant ... I like you as more than a friend and it's just ... really confusing for me."

Fuck, that makes me happy. Even though I won't push her for more, it feels good to know that I'm not the only one who feels the attraction between us. I tamp down on the joy that overwhelms me, though. The last thing I want to do is get overly excited and scare her off.

"I was with Tommy for a long time," she goes on. "Our relationship was filled with very high highs and very low lows. I loved him a lot, but after a while, I realized it wasn't a sustainable kind of love. If we'd ended up engaged, married, it would've never lasted. When a connection is right, it shouldn't be that rocky. Eventually, I'd had enough."

"What happened?" It's none of my business, but my curiosity has gotten the best of me. "What was the turning point?"

She frowns, looking apprehensive.

If she doesn't want to talk about it, I won't push it. I consider telling her to forget I asked, but before I can, she takes a deep breath and straightens in the booth.

"He asked me to go to a party. I really didn't want to go, but I agreed. To keep the peace." She lowers her head, focused on her plate for a moment, then locks her eyes with mine again. "I showed up late and found him flirting with another girl. He did that a lot. When I annoyed him. To punish me or something, I guess. That time, I just … I'd had enough. I marched up to him and told him that I was done. But the next morning…" She shook her head. "He was texting me like nothing had changed. Like he was sure I'd be over it. I guess I can't blame him for thinking that since I took him back so many times. But I meant it."

My chest tightens at the hint of pain in her voice. "Good for you. You deserve better, and I'm sure that wasn't easy."

"It wasn't." She bites her lip, her gaze averted. "It

sounds so pathetic, but I think because of my parents, I learned not to expect much from relationships."

"It's not pathetic," I insist. God damn, this girl's upbringing really was shitty. It's really true what they say. Money *isn't* everything.

It hurts, knowing she's never been loved properly. Not by her parents and not by doucheface Tommy. Bertie deserved better from all of them.

"I hope…" I inhale deeply and let the breath out slowly, gathering myself. "I hope that when you're ready to open your heart up again, you find someone capable of loving you the way you deserve."

She tugs on the ends of her hair, head lowered. "Thank you."

Straightening, I pick up my burger. Only then do I realize how much time has passed. Shit. I have about five minutes left in my break.

"What's wrong?" she asks.

"I have to get back to work in a few minutes." I take a giant bite of my burger, determined to finish it before I'm out of time. I won't have another break until the shift I'm covering ends.

"Oh," she breathes. "I'm so sorry. I shouldn't have been so chatty."

Frowning, I lean in closer, burger still in hand. "Don't ever be sorry for talking to me. I love it."

We eat in silence for the next couple of minutes. I'm wiping my hands on a napkin, getting ready to get up and get back to work, when my mom appears at the side of the table.

My heart lurches as I look up at her. *Oh no.*

"Hi." She smiles at Bertie. "I'm Luke's mom. Jocelyn."

"I'm Bertie. It's nice to meet you." She extends a hand and smiles.

Mom slides her palm against Bertie's, head tilted in interest. "That's an unusual name."

"It's short for Beatrice."

"You didn't want to go by Bea?"

I shoot my mom a look, silently willing her to stop interrogating Bertie. I'm sure she can feel the death glare, but she ignores me.

Bertie shrugs. "I've gone by Bertie since I was a little girl. I've never thought about changing it."

"I like it. It suits you," my mom says, her smile warm. "I thought I'd pop over and see if you have plans for Christmas Eve. Are you spending it with family or...?"

I'm fairly certain my ears are bright red based on how hot they feel.

Bertie's shoulders slump. "No, I'm alone for the holiday this year."

My mom's reaction is the opposite. Her whole face lights up like this is good news. "You should spend it with us, then. Come over for Christmas Eve dinner. You can even stay the night if you want. No one should be alone on Christmas."

With my hands covering my face, I hang my head. Is my mother seriously playing wingman right now?

Bertie smiles. "That would be lovely. Luke asked me, but I hadn't had the chance to tell him yes yet."

My mom's smile only grows. "That's my Luke. Such a good boy."

"Mom." I stifle a groan. "You make me sound like a dog, not your son."

She ignores me, her body turned so it's facing Bertie only. "I look forward to having you. Is there any particular dish or dessert you enjoy?"

Cheeks pink, Bertie shakes her head. "Whatever you make will be lovely."

"All right." My mom nods, the gears turning in her head. "I'll see you then. It was good to meet you, Bertie."

"You, too."

My mom heads back to the counter with an extra pep in her step. Dammit. I'll never hear the end of this.

"Your mom is nice," Bertie says, smiling at her back.

She means it, too. There isn't even a trace of sarcasm in her tone.

"She is. I'm sorry about that."

"It's fine." She waves off my concern. "I really was going to take you up on your offer."

"You were?" I straighten, surprised.

She nods. "Yeah, I've been working up the courage to text you. It feels a little pathetic to beg to spend the holiday with a family that isn't mine."

"It's not pathetic, and besides, I asked you, remember?" I eye the time and groan. "I've got to get back to work."

"Okay. Thanks for sitting with me."

With a nod, I gather up my plate and drink to take to the back.

As I pass her, my mom bumps her hip into mine. "You're welcome," she singsongs, shooting a triumphant smile my way.

If, by some miracle, this turns into something, she'll never let me live it down.

FIVE

Bertie

I'M A BALL OF NERVES AS I PACE MY DORM ROOM, waiting for Luke to pick me up.

It's silly, really, that I'm on the verge of panicking. I already met his mom, and she was plenty nice. I have no reason to think that tonight will be anything but lovely.

As I assess my appearance in my floor-length mirror again, I frown. Maybe my pale blue turtleneck sweater was a bad choice. Suddenly, I worry it washes me out. And I'm reconsidering my hair.

Would it look better down? I'm about to reach up to take it out of its ponytail when he texts that he's outside.

Letting out a breath, I text back.

> Me: I'll be right down.

> Luke: I'm already on my way up.

With shaky hands, I swipe my purse off my bed, and when I open the door, I find him already walking down the hallway.

"Hey," he says, the dimple in his cheek flashing at me. "Are you ready, or do you need more time?"

"I'm ready." I pick up the bouquet and wine from the table, along with a nice box of chocolates. They're all for his mom, though there's a small gift for him stuffed in my purse.

"What's all that?" he asks, motioning to the items I'm juggling.

"Oh." My stomach twists at his scrutiny. *Maybe I shouldn't have gotten anything?* "This is for your mom. I didn't want to show up empty-handed. Please tell me she isn't allergic to flowers, wine, or chocolate. If she is, I might cry."

He takes the wine bottle, gently cradling it in the crook of one arm, then the flowers. "She's not allergic.

That's kind of you, B. I promise, she didn't expect you to bring anything."

Now that I've got a free hand, I adjust my purse strap. "It doesn't feel right not to."

Luke looks me up and down, and for a split-second, I'm back to worrying that my outfit is terrible and I should've changed.

"You look pretty."

Oh.

Oh.

"Thank you."

"I like you in blue."

He likes me in blue.

I think I might be swooning. How absolutely pathetic. What's even more pathetic is how I can't remember Tommy ever telling me I looked pretty. When I was in the thick of the relationship, I suppose I didn't think about those things. Now that I'm out of it, I can't believe I accepted so little.

"The blue looks good?" I smooth a hand down my abdomen, over the sweater I was doubting only minutes ago.

He grins, nodding. "You look good in anything, but I've officially become partial to you in blue."

A zing of pleasure moves through me at his appreciation. I have a feeling I'll be splurging and ordering more things in blue if only to hear him compliment me.

"Need to grab anything else?"

I shake my head and step out into the hall. "Nope, this is it."

Once my door is locked, we head down the eerily quiet hall. From what I can tell, there are only a handful of us left in the whole building.

Outside, Luke leads me to an older red and white truck. Despite its age, it's well taken care of, and the paint shines in the late afternoon light.

As he opens the passenger door for me, he looks away, his head lowered a fraction. "I'm sure it's not what you're used to, but it gets me around."

With a hand on his forearm, I wait for him to look at me, then give him a genuine smile. "I love it."

I'm not just saying it to make him feel better either. It's sturdy, with character. The interior smells like him, with a hint of mint and tobacco mixed into the leather.

"Thanks." He smiles, ducking his head.

He rounds the hood, and once he's seated beside me, he starts up the truck and turns the volume down on the radio.

Once again, we fall into a comfortable silence. It's amazing, how easy this is for us. After only a few minutes, he turns into a neighborhood filled with older homes. I keep my expression neutral as we roll slowly down the street. They're the kind of places—shutters hanging off siding, overgrown lawns, gravel drives overrun with weeds—that would send my parents into cardiac arrest.

Luke turns down another street that ends in a cul-de-sac and pulls into the driveway of a small ranch with white siding and a red front door. It's the most put together house I've seen since we turned into the neighborhood. Christmas lights decorate the eaves, and the front door boasts a cheerful wreath with a Santa Claus hat.

The house could probably fit into my family's living room, but I love it before I even set foot inside. It's clear, even from the driveway, that happy people live here.

Luke shoots me a nervous look as he shuts the truck off. "It's not much, but it's home."

"It's perfect," I say softly.

He regards me for a moment, his lips turned down, but that expression turns into a smile when he realizes I'm being serious.

He gets out and is around to open my door before I have a chance to unbuckle and collect my things.

"Don't be nervous," he tells me. It's scary how easily he can read me.

He takes the flowers and wine from me again, then

helps me out. Once I'm steady and the door is shut, he grabs my hand and guides me to the house. Perhaps I should shake off the hold, but I don't. It's pointless anyway, because he drops it a moment later to open a side door.

We step right into a kitchen, the smell of which is heavenly.

I must hum in approval, because Luke shoots me a knowing smile.

The woman from the diner steps away from a pan of macaroni and cheese, and with a beaming smile, she throws her arms around me. It's embarrassing, the way I melt into her hug. Neither of my parents has ever hugged me like this. For show, sure, but not because they simply wanted to hold me and wrap me in comfort.

When she releases me, I take the flowers and wine from Luke. "I brought these for you."

Her blue eyes dance with genuine pleasure. "Oh, how sweet of you. Thank you. Lukie"—she raises a brow at her son—"would you mind putting these in a vase for me?"

Lukie. I try not to smile at the nickname.

"Thank you again for having me. I ... it really means a lot to me." Flushing, I choke back the emotion threatening to spill out of me.

Despite my best effort to remain composed, Luke looks back over his shoulder at me, frowning in concern.

"We're glad you could join us." Jocelyn squeezes my hand. "Go ahead and take a seat. I have a few things to finish up."

Lips pressed together, I survey the kitchen. "Do you need any help? I'm not much of a cook, but I can ... stir or something."

Luke, who's now carefully arranging the flowers in a vase, chuckles.

"That would be great." Jocelyn takes my hand and guides me over to the counter. "I haven't seasoned the mashed potatoes yet. All the ingredients are right there."

She points everything out and leaves me to my own devices.

I add the butter and what looks like chives and garlic before stirring with a wooden spoon. With as thick as the potatoes are, I get in a good arm workout. While I do my best to distribute the seasoning evenly, I survey the space around me. Luke wasn't kidding—there's way more food than the three of us can eat.

The kitchen is tiny, so we bump into each other occasionally, but no one makes a fuss. Festive music plays softly on a radio in the corner. It feels like I've been transported into one of my favorite Christmas movies. It's so sweet. So perfect. And the best part is, not one interaction or a single word is forced.

Jocelyn asks me about my interests, what I'm studying, my plans for after I graduate. Each question is asked with genuine care rather than out of obligation. She's such a stark contrast to my parents. She's pure warmth and sunshine, while being in their presence is like being stranded in an icy rainstorm.

By the time we sit to eat, all my nerves have disappeared. I don't feel like an outsider at all with the two of them. Not for the first time since we arrived, I'm thankful that despite my doubts, I agreed to come tonight. This is far better than wallowing in my dorm with Kraft mac 'n' cheese.

This is a *family*.

An ache settles deep inside me.

This is what I want one day.

A family of my own to sit down and have meals with.

A house filled with music, laughter, and conversation.

A husband who showers me with kisses and kids that groan about it.

"Is everything okay?" Jocelyn asks, nodding at my plate, where I'm pushing around the broccoli casserole.

"It's great." I smile, and it's not forced at all. "Just got lost in my thoughts."

Luke watches me with those blue eyes that see too much.

"Everything is fantastic," I say, stabbing a hunk of broccoli. "You're a great cook."

Jocelyn smiles, her eyes crinkling at the corners. "That's very kind of you."

"Just wait until you have her apple pie with homemade vanilla ice cream." Luke holds my gaze in a way that makes my stomach dip.

Doing my best to ignore the sensation, I clear my throat. "That sounds fantastic. I'm not sure I'll have room."

"I was thinking," Jocelyn says, her smile a tad mischievous, "why don't you stay the night?"

"Oh." I shake my head, my heart lurching a bit. "I couldn't impose like that."

Luke lets out a groan. "Mom."

"You can take Luke's room." She straightens, her shoulders pulled back. "It won't be any trouble at all. He can sleep on the couch."

"No, no." I shake my head. "I promise you, I'm fine."

Luke shoots me an apologetic look, but Jocelyn is not one to be deterred.

"You shouldn't be alone on Christmas," she says. "Please, it'll make me feel better to have you here."

"I…" I bite my lip, feeling cornered while simultaneously wanting to stay. But it's ridiculous, right? She doesn't know me.

"Just think about it," she says, gently putting me out of my misery.

After dinner, I offer to help clean up, but Jocelyn shoos the two of us out of the kitchen and into the family room.

Once we're alone, Luke rubs his hand against the back of his head, his closely cropped hair rasping against his palm. "I'm really sorry about her."

"Don't be." I settle my butt on the couch, and instantly, a small moan falls out of my lips. Wow. This has to be the softest, most comfortable couch I've ever sat on. The tan piece of furniture is big and thick, and in no world would it be considered stylish, but what it lacks in looks, it makes up for in comfort.

Luke arches a brow at me, lips twitching with amusement.

"I've never sat on a couch this comfy before."

He huffs a laugh. "Big Lots special."

"I've never been to a Big Lots." I rub my fingers over the soft fabric, noting the way the color shifts slightly when I move one way, then shifts back when I move the other.

"That so?" He sounds surprised, but quickly shakes

his head. "Of course you haven't. Sometimes I forget you're…" He gestures at me.

"A Carthwright?" I finish for him.

"Yeah." He sighs.

Pressing my palms into the cushion on either side of me, I peer up at him. "Would you take me sometime?"

He grimaces. "To Big Lots?"

"Yes."

The furrow in his brow deepens. "You really want to go? It's not that great."

"I want to go."

"Okay." He draws out the word like maybe he's doubting my sanity. "I could take you other places."

I fight a smile. "Like where?"

"I don't know." He picks up the remote, his lips quirking. "Outback, maybe? I'm guessing you've never had a bloomin' onion."

"Definitely not." There's no stopping the grin now.

"Woman." He drops his head back with a groan. "You haven't lived."

I think we're flirting, but I'm not quite sure. I'm greatly out of practice.

"I'll take you," he murmurs. "But not as a date. I know you don't want that."

"Right." My smile evaporates, and I lower my head. I

did say that I didn't want to date, so why am I practically on my knees begging him to spend time with me?

"Any preferences on movies?" he asks, kneeling on the floor in front of the TV.

"What do you have?"

"Um..." He opens a cabinet door, revealing rows of DVDs. Humming, he pulls a few out, then holds them up for me to see. "These. Or we could rent something on TV."

"*Unaccompanied Minors*." I read the title on one. "Let's do that."

With a nod, he pops it into the DVD player.

Jocelyn pokes her head into the family room, eyes ping-ponging between the two of us. "Go ahead and start a movie, you two. I'm going to hop into the shower first."

Luke narrows his eyes at her, as if silently saying *I see you and I know exactly what you're doing*.

Undeterred, she smiles, then turns and disappears down the hall.

"Sorry about her." He stands from the floor and puts his hands on his hips. "She likes to meddle."

"I like it. I like *her*." And I mean it. "I wish I had a mom who cared that much about me."

He rubs his jaw. "Don't worry. If you let her, she'll take you under her wing." With a shake of his head, he settles into the recliner a few feet away, and while I think it's sweet he's trying to keep his distance, I stupidly want him closer.

"I don't bite," I tease, patting the empty spot on the couch beside me.

He arches a perfectly shaped brow. It's annoying how well-manicured they look when I highly doubt he's ever taken tweezers or wax to them. Meanwhile, I have to brush my eyebrow hair every morning so it's not sticking in every direction.

Silently, he gets up and joins me on the couch.

I'm not sure what I'm doing, tempting fate like this, but I can't help but revel in his closeness.

"Have you heard from your parents today?" Luke asks while a preview plays on the TV.

Hands clasped in my lap, I shake my head. "No. I didn't expect to."

He frowns, a flash of irritation momentarily marring his handsome face. "They suck."

"They do," I agree. There's no point in arguing that point.

We're about thirty minutes into the movie when Jocelyn joins us with plates of apple pie and ice cream.

The sound that comes out of me at my first taste is downright ungodly. Holding my breath, I duck to hide my heated cheeks.

Luke gives me a little smirk. "Told you it was good."

"I'm so happy you like it," Jocelyn says, a proud smile on her lips.

"Could you teach me to make this?" I point at the dessert with my fork, as if she doesn't know what I'm talking about.

"Sure," she agrees. "I'd love to. Luke cooks, but he's not much into baking."

He looks over at me with a sigh. "Because cooking can be experimental, and baking is precise. I don't do well with precise."

When the movie finishes, Luke stands and stretches his arms above his head, flashing a glimpse of his taut, tanned stomach. His olive skin tone makes him look tan all year round, especially compared to my pale complexion.

Heart skipping at the sight of him, I turn my head slightly. As I do, I catch Jocelyn watching me. When she smirks, I want to melt into the couch.

"The offer is still on the table if you want to stay the night." She eases up from the chair and shuffles closer to her son. "It's up to you. I'm going to bed. Merry Christmas Eve." She has to stand on her tiptoes to get her arms around Luke's neck. Once she's pressed a kiss to his cheek, she lowers herself and steps over to me. "And Merry Christmas Eve to you, too, Bertie." She hugs me, and then she's gone.

Luke shoves his hands into his pockets, facing me with a thin-lipped smile. "Have you decided what you want to do?"

"What do you want me to do?" I counter.

Shoulders drooping, he sighs. "Nuh-uh. If you want to stay, you have to make the decision."

I wring my hands, scanning the room, taking in the small Christmas tree. "It feels weird for me to stay…"

"But?" he prompts, a hopeful glint in his eye.

"I … I like the idea of staying," I say, suddenly hit with the urge to cry. "I really don't want to be alone on Christmas."

Taking my hand, he pulls me off the couch and into his arms. As his heart beats a steady rhythm against my ear, I let out a sigh, feeling more content than I think I ever have.

"You'll stay in my room," he says, lips brushing the top of my head. "I changed the sheets this morning."

"No." I shake my head and pull back. "I don't want you to have to sleep on the couch."

"I'll be all right," he promises, lacing our fingers together.

Without giving me another moment to argue, he leads me down the hall to his room. It's clean and smells like him. On one wall, there's a corkboard full of childhood pictures and small hockey memorabilia. The comforter is a light blue color and looks incredibly soft. Like it's been washed a million times and is perfectly worn in.

He rifles through the top drawer of his dresser and procures a t-shirt.

Turning, he hands it to me. "This should be comfy enough for you to sleep in."

I hold it up, relishing the soft fabric beneath my fingertips. It's a hockey shirt, with his last name on the back and the school crest and his first name on the front right breast area.

I arch a brow, holding it up in front of me. "Plastering your name on me, I see."

His cheeks pinken. "It's old."

"It's got to be less than almost four years old."

He wets his lips with his tongue, the move snagging my attention and making my breath catch. "I can find something else."

I shake my head and pull the shirt into my chest. "No, this is good."

"I'll, uh…" He rubs his hands together. "Leave you to it." He winces at his words. "That sounded weird." Shaking his head, he says, "Remote for the TV and fan are beside the bed. If you need anything, just text me."

I take a step toward him, still clutching the shirt. "I can sleep on the couch. I promise I'll be okay."

Looming over me, he scowls. "Not a chance, B. Good night." His expression smooths out, and his lips part, like maybe he wants to say something else, but instead, he lets himself out of the room and closes the door lightly behind him.

I pull my phone from my pocket and reply to a few texts from friends, then shoot one off to my mom and dad, saying I hope they're having a good time. Even though I secretly hope they're miserable, because fuck them.

Finished with my messages, I toss my phone onto Luke's bed, then carefully undress and fold my clothes. As I tug his shirt over my head, I'm practically drowning in his scent. Is it cologne? Or is it his own unique scent? I wish I knew. Either way, though, I can't help but be drawn to it.

In search of the bathroom, I ease the bedroom door open. As I'm peering into the hall, the door across from me opens, and steam billows out, practically thick enough to knock me backward.

Then Luke emerges.

Bare-chested.

Wet.

In only a towel.

I squeeze my thighs together. It's been so long since

I've had anything other than my vibrator, and my body is reminding me of that fact right now.

"Hey," he says. "I, uh, I forgot to grab my sleep clothes."

All I can do is blink up at him and watch as a droplet of water runs down his pec and over his abs. When I force my focus back to his face, he breaks out in a slow grin.

"Bertie, I need to get around you."

"Oh." I swallow. "Right." On shaky legs, I step aside. "I was coming to brush my teeth. Do you have any spare toothbrushes?"

"Under the sink," he answers with his back to me as he pulls clothes out of the dresser.

Before I get caught staring again, I spin and lock myself in the bathroom. Though I'm engulfed in his scent—not only from his t-shirt now, but his soap as well—I force myself to ignore the way it makes my pulse race. I do my business, then brush my teeth with the new toothbrush I found right where he said it would be and the toothpaste that rests on the sink.

The hall is dark when I step out and tiptoe toward the family room, where Luke is laying a sheet over the couch cushions.

"Thanks for the toothbrush."

He looks up, a blanket clasped in his hands. "It's no problem."

I wring my fingers together and swallow past the lump in my throat. "Well, good night, I guess."

I don't know what makes me add the *I guess* part.

He smiles, amusement in his eyes. "Good night, B."

I give an awkward wave—because of course I do—and make my way back to his room.

With the TV on for background noise, I climb into his bed. His mattress is soft, worn in like it's made to curve around his much bigger body. It's like I'm lying in a hole, but it's comforting, soothing, being enveloped like this.

Despite how good it feels, I'm plagued with guilt, because while I'm in here, he's crammed onto that small couch. There's no way he actually fits. And as much as I long for his company right now, I can't bring myself to text him and ask him to sleep—only sleep—in here with me.

I'm too afraid of being rejected.

Six

Luke

I'VE BEEN STARING AT THE CEILING FOR WHAT HAS to be a couple of hours. I've refused to check the time, though, so I can't be certain.

Normally, I have no problem with sleep. I'm usually worn out from school and practice, so by the time my head hits the pillow, I'm out.

My struggle tonight has nothing to do with being on the couch and everything to do with the woman in my bed.

I press the heels of my hands to my eyes.

Just friends. She doesn't want more than that.

Fuck, is it hard to think that way when she looks at me the way she did several times tonight. Her eyes full of heat, her cheeks pink. She wants me, that's obvious. But she's afraid of commitment. And after her ex, how can I blame her?

Sure, we could have a purely physical relationship, but I want more, and I'm scared if I give in and take what I can get, I'll lose any chance of a real connection with her in the future.

Though what future do we really have?

If I'm drafted like I hope to be, I'll be gone, living in another city so I can play hockey. And though we discussed the future at dinner, the details of where Bertie sees herself next year were vague.

The devil on my shoulder urges me to sneak back to my room and see if she's as worked up as I am.

Tamping down the urge, I blow out a breath and roll over to face the wall.

"Luke?"

The single syllable is so quiet I almost miss it.

But the next words are a little louder and a little closer. "Luke, are you awake?"

I sit up, blanket falling to my waist, and find Bertie shadowed in the archway.

"Are you okay?" I look her over, but it's dark and hard to make out more than her silhouette.

She nods in the darkness. "I'm fine."

"Do you need water or something?" I shift and swing my legs over the side of the couch.

A shake of her head in response. "I'm having trouble sleeping."

"Oh. Do you ... I can take you back to your dorm. Would that help?"

Another shake of her head. "Will you lay with me?"

With that one simple question, I swear my dick comes awake.

"Um ... I'm not sure that's a good idea."

Shoulders falling, she creeps closer, her figure more prominent now that she's not bathed in heavy shadows.

"Fuck," I mutter to myself, low enough she won't hear.

Tossing the blanket off, I heave myself up. Then I shuffle over to her and take her small hand in mine. It's cool to the touch.

Quietly, I lead her back to my room, and without a word, we get into the bed together.

She takes the side closer to the wall, putting me in my usual spot. We end up on our sides, my body spooned around hers.

Damn, it feels way too good to hold her like this.

The sweetest torture.

"You're hard."

I groan. "Sorry. Can't help it. Just ignore it. It'll go away eventually."

Her laughter shakes us both, which doesn't help my dick one bit.

"Bertie," I warn softly, my lips brushing the back of her neck.

She giggles again. "Oops."

I press my hand to her stomach to still her. It isn't until she lets out a tiny gasp that I realize the intimacy of the move. But I don't let go.

"You know what you're doing," I warn her.

"Sorry." She doesn't sound sorry at all. "No funny business. I promise."

Silence falls between us, thick with sexual tension.

Internally, I'm spiraling. I shouldn't have given in and come back here with her.

"Luke?"

"Mhm?" I hum.

"I really want you to touch me."

I sigh against her ear, my heart lurching even as I get harder. "Bertie."

"Please."

"You're not being fair."

"I'm sorry," she apologizes again, this time slipping

her hand over mine on her abdomen. "Ignore me. But please don't leave."

"I want to touch you," I tell her, whispering the confession against the shell of her ear. "But then I'm afraid you'll ignore me."

"I wouldn't do that." She wiggles against me, though this time, I'm not sure she registers the subtle movement.

"So if I slip my hand under this shirt and into your panties," I say, easing the cotton covering her and running my fingers along the waistband of her underwear, "you're still going to talk to me after?"

"Yes." The word is a breathy gasp.

My stomach tightens with need. "Are you wet, B?"

Another wiggle of her butt.

"B?" I prompt when she doesn't answer.

"Yes."

I bite my lip to hide my smile. Not that she can see it anyway. "Were you wet when you came out to find me? Were you laying in my bed thinking about me?"

"Y-Yes," she whimpers.

"Fuck, baby." I kiss her shoulder where the shirt has drifted down to reveal her smooth, creamy skin. "I'm not going to fuck you," I tell her. "But I will get you off." I slip my fingers beneath her panties and circle her clit, pulling a gasp from her lips. When I dip lower, she moans.

"You're fucking soaked. Just thinking about me gets you this wet, huh?"

She whimpers, rolling her ass against my dick.

"You don't have to answer me," I croon against her neck, rubbing her clit. "I already know it does."

"Luke," she breathes, the sound full of need and desire.

Fuck, what I'd give to hear her say my name again. But we're not alone in the house.

I slip a finger inside her, and she gasps again. Sliding my other arm beneath her neck, I cover her mouth with my hand.

"You gotta be quiet, B. I can't have you waking up my mom, can I?"

She whimpers again, and I swear she gets even wetter, like the idea of being caught excites her. It's an interesting development. I never would have guessed she'd be the type to enjoy that kind of thing.

My girl is full of surprises.

She rocks against my hand, making the sweetest little noises beneath my palm.

Pressing my lips against the crook of her neck, I suck at her delicate skin. "Your pussy is squeezing the life out of my fingers." I pull my hand from her mouth and slip it down the front of her t-shirt. "So fucking needy for me, aren't you, baby?"

"Yes. Please. More."

"More what?" I tease.

She turns her head, peering at me over her shoulder as best as she can. Her eyes are hazy with lust, and I fucking love that I'm the one who put that look there.

"I want you."

I brush my nose against her cheek. "You've got me."

She has no idea the hold she has on me. I've been gone for this girl since freshman year. True, I didn't pine after her like a lovesick puppy, but I never forgot her.

"Please, fuck me," she begs, reaching back to rub her hand over my hard cock where it strains against my pants.

"I told you I wouldn't."

She whimpers like she's in pain. "Luke."

"Trust me, I want to." I press my thumb against her clit, and she cries out, making me consider covering her mouth again. "But I'm selfish, and I want you to be mine before I do."

It's not like I haven't had sex for the sake of enjoyment, but Bertie is different. I *like* her. I don't want to get hurt because I feel more for her than she does me.

"I want you," she confesses on a breath. "Even though I shouldn't."

She shouldn't? Whatever that means. I don't think she's talking about the difference in our social status.

Bertie might be from one of the wealthiest families in the US, but she's also humble and down-to-earth.

Rather than respond, I continue teasing her with my hand, pressing kisses to her neck, and nipping at the sensitive skin there. The room fills with her panting breaths, making it clear that she's close.

At her first cry, I cover her mouth again. I desperately want to hear her, but my mom is a light sleeper, and even though she's made it obvious she wants Bertie and me involved, I don't exactly think she needs to be privy to what we're up to in here.

The roll of her hips slows as she comes down from the high, and as her cries quiet, I let my hand drift away from her mouth. Her breaths are heavy, her body limp, spent.

I pull my fingers from her and rub the wetness around her swollen clit.

She's still twitching at the sensation when she rolls over to face me with a smile. "Your turn."

I shake my head, and as her face falls in response, my heart clenches. Damn, I hate that my rejection has hurt her. "No." I tuck a piece of blond hair behind her ear. "If you touch me right now, I won't be able to stop until I'm inside you."

She grins, touching my cheek with a gentle finger. "I wouldn't mind."

I know she wouldn't. And fuck if it doesn't take all my self-control to hold back.

"I'll be okay," I tell her. "Try to go to sleep."

She looks like she's going to protest, but before she can, she's hit with a surprise yawn. "Fine. But just know, I give an A-plus blow job."

"I know you do."

She gives me a sleepy, satisfied smile. "Aw, you remember."

I chuckle, making her body shake with mine. "Of course I remember." I think about that night far more than I'd like to admit. If she knew how much, she'd probably bolt.

"Go to sleep." I wrap my arm around her.

With a hum, she settles her head on my chest, her fingers splayed against my stomach.

I close my eyes, and for a moment, I let myself imagine that this is real and I get to hold her every night.

SEVEN

Bertie

My dorm is too quiet, too empty after spending the day with Luke and his mom. Jocelyn asked me to stay a second night, and while I was tempted, I knew I couldn't. The last thing I need is to embarrass myself again by begging Luke to fuck me like I did last night.

He might be the only single guy I know who isn't down for unattached sex.

And ... I like that about him.

Even if it frustrates me to no end and has my libido crying out in desperation.

I set the Tupperware container of food Jocelyn sent me home with on the counter and shrug out of my coat. Tossing the garment onto the back of the couch, I head for the bathroom. Showering will not only kill some time this evening, but with any luck, it'll help me put off the feeling of utter loneliness that's bound to hit me.

While the water heats, I typically remove by makeup, but since I stayed at Luke's, I've been bare-faced all day. So while I wait, I pull up a music app and turn on my Bluetooth speaker, then I get undressed and toss my clothes into the hamper I keep in the corner.

I've always loved showers, spending way more time in them than I should. Rosie used to get annoyed with my hour-long rituals.

Unfortunately, the long shower does little to distract me from my thoughts about Luke.

He's got me all tied up in knots, making it feel impossible to stick to my no-dating mantra, because I *like* him, and the more time I spend with him, the deeper that like goes.

If I'd asked him to stay and hang out tonight, I have no doubt he would have. But after dinner with him and his mother yesterday and spending the entirety of today with them, it felt imperative that I put some separation between us.

Once I've pulled on a cozy set of pajamas, I check my messages, finding Merry Christmas texts and others of the sort. I'm hurt, but not surprised, to find nothing from either of my parents.

An afterthought, that's all I am to them. For years, nothing more than a cute accessory to show off to their rich friends. A way to say *look at us. We're wealthy and powerful and we procreated to make this super baby offspring*. Now that I'm an adult, they clearly don't need me anymore.

Darkness comes early these days, and while I shouldn't feel so exhausted after doing nothing but sitting on the couch while Luke and his mom exchanged gifts, then lounging while watching Christmas movies, there's nothing I want more than to climb into my bed.

It's safe to say my exhaustion is more emotional than physical.

No one's life is rainbows and sunshine, I get that, but from what I've witnessed, Luke and his mom live a relatively happy one. All my life, I've been surrounded by families like mine, but I always knew there had to be better out there, and over the last twenty-four hours or so, the Coveys showed it to me.

My father got my mom a Birkin for Christmas one

year, and she tossed it carelessly aside. I think I've seen her carry it once in the last decade.

Luke got his mom a cute pair of mittens, and her eyes lit up like he'd given her a rare, valuable artifact.

Why can't you give him a chance? I plead with myself.

Because I'm scared. Breaking up with Tommy for good was painful, but if things ended with Luke, I'd be devastated.

I'm not sure I'd ever recover. Because Luke would care for me in a way I've never been cared for before.

Of course, as if he can sense that I'm thinking about him, a text message comes through.

> Luke: Hey. Just wanted to check in and see if you're okay.

I bite my lip, willing my heart not to leap at his consideration and kindness.

> Me: I'm fine. Showered and getting in bed.

An instant later, my phone rings, startling me so badly I nearly drop it. Luke's name flashes on my screen.

"Hello?" I answer, stomach flipping.

He groans, the sound pure sin. "Bertie, did you have to tell me that?"

"What?" I ask, racking my brain for the issue in my simple statement.

"Shower. You. Naked and wet."

"Oh."

"Yeah, oh." He gives a soft chuckle. "You truly have no idea what you do to me, do you?"

Warmth unfurls in my core at the thought. I shouldn't say it. I shouldn't let my curiosity get the best of me. But there's no stopping it. "What do I do to you?"

He lets out a resigned sigh, making the line crackle. I don't know where he is, but in my mind, I picture him in his bed, leaning against the headboard.

"You make me crazy in the best way. Fuck, I hope this doesn't sound creepy, but I think about you a lot. More than I should. I wonder what you're doing, if you ate breakfast, what your favorite coffee flavor is, favorite season, favorite color. What you like to read. Your favorite movie. If you've slept well." He groans. "You have me twisted in knots without even trying."

I breathe in and out slowly, trying to process his words, my hands suddenly shaking. "Wow," I whisper.

He huffs. "I'm sorry. That was a lot."

"No, it's okay." I brush my hair off my forehead. "Right now I'm getting in bed like I said. It's kind of cold and empty without you. I know it was only one night, but

I liked sleeping with you. I did eat breakfast—you were there for it."

He chuckles at that, a rough sound that sends shivers down my spine.

"My favorite coffee flavor changes, but my go-to right now is a peppermint mocha. My favorite season is fall. I love wearing oversized sweatshirts and watching the leaves change. My favorite color is pink. I don't read much, but when I do, it's romance and usually dirty."

This time, his laugh is bigger, deeper.

"My favorite movie is a hard one. Right now, it's probably *The Holiday*, but frankly, anything Nancy Meyers is involved in is a masterpiece. I did sleep well last night. Better than I have in a while. I think I have my bed partner and an earth-shattering orgasm to thank for that. And you have me twisted in knots, too." I whisper the last part, the confession falling off my lips more easily than I thought it would. "You scare me."

"Well, fuck. That doesn't sound good."

My stomach sinks at the defeat in his tone. "I don't mean like that. It's just ... breaking up with Tommy was hard enough. You? I think you could ruin me."

I can't believe I'm being this brutally honest with him. I've obviously lost my mind.

He's quiet for so long that I pull my phone away from my ear to make sure the call is still connected.

Finally, he speaks, his voice hoarse. "If I ever have the pleasure of being the recipient of your heart, I promise I'll care for it better than my own. I will never hurt you, Bertie."

I close my eyes, soaking in the truth of his words.

Still, the fear that grips me tightens. "I better go to bed."

He lets out a soft sigh, as if he isn't ready to hang up, but he doesn't argue. "All right, good night."

Holding back a sniffle, I say "night" and disconnect the call.

EIGHT

Luke

BERTIE AND I DIDN'T SPEAK AT ALL YESTERDAY.

I've tried not to read too much into it, though it's hard, considering I admitted just how much I like her. So it comes as a surprise when I open the door and find her standing on the front porch.

"Hi," she says softly, the tip of her nose pink. "I hope it's okay I showed up like this. I saw your truck was in the driveway so…" She peeks over her shoulder, and when she turns back, she's frowning. "I can go."

Before she can turn and leave, I grasp her wrist. "Stay."

God, I sound like I'm begging.

I *am* begging.

She comes inside, hovering in the doorway and peering down at the snow and mud clinging to the bottom of her shoes. Cringing, she looks up at me. "I should've taken my shoes off on the porch. I'm sorry. I'll clean it up."

"It's okay," I insist, way too giddy to be in her proximity. She could dump a truckload of snow in the living room, and it wouldn't sour my mood.

With a deep breath, I rein myself in. I can't react this way every time I see her—like an excited puppy jumping at her legs.

"I ... uh ... I realized I forgot to give you your Christmas present." She reaches into her bag and pulls out a small box. "I don't know how I didn't think of it. I guess because I was enjoying the day, it slipped my mind."

I stare at her, mouth open, more than a little surprised. "I ... I didn't get you anything."

She laughs, the sound light and airy. Completely unbothered. "I didn't expect you to."

"B-but..." I stutter, at a loss for words. "You got me something."

She shrugs. "It's something you need."

"Something I need?" I murmur, taking the package from her. As I study it, I rub my fingers over the shiny green paper with multi-colored strands of Christmas lights on it.

"Yeah." She shrugs again.

It's cute, how nervous she is. It gives me hope that perhaps her feelings are growing for me.

"I saw them and thought of you."

My grin is instantaneous. "You were thinking about me?"

She rolls her eyes. "Of course that's what you took from that."

"Hey." My smile gets even bigger, and I swear my heart expands. "You said it. Not me."

When she purses her lips and bends to remove her boots, I have to fight the urge to pump my fist. She's staying, and there was no begging involved.

When she straightens, she brushes the hair away from her face. "Just open the present."

I tear through the paper and stare in disbelief at the box no bigger than my palm.

"Bertie." Her name is a soft exhale. "This is ... too much. These are almost three hundred dollars."

"It's not too much. You use earbuds all the time, don't you? I always see you with the pair that only work with your phone if you have an adapter. These work with Bluetooth and have noise cancellation."

Unbidden, tears prick at the backs of my eyes.

Dammit. It's not about the gift.

It's her thoughtfulness. She noticed my old, ratty earbuds and how often I use them. She doesn't even know that I have OCD and struggle with racing thoughts. She doesn't realize that music helps center me, helps calm me down when I start to spiral and things get to be too much. But she *sees* me.

"It's okay, right?" She sounds worried now. "You look upset."

"You have no idea how much a gift like this means to me." I stuff the small box of Apple AirPods—something I would never spend my own money on, since I help my mom with the bills and food—into my pocket. Then I cup her face and kiss her.

I don't even think about it. It's second nature to slant my mouth over hers.

She tastes like peppermint, like maybe she had one of those peppermint mochas she loves on her way over here.

She kisses me back, a small moan leaving her as she stretches up on her toes and winds her arms around my neck, her breasts pressing against my chest through her open coat.

It happens naturally, the way I pick her up and her legs go around my waist.

I don't even think as I carry her back to my room and carefully strip her of her clothes.

"Are you sure about this?" she asks, naked beneath me as I roll a condom on.

"I'm sure."

I kiss her, savoring the way her mouth feels against mine. I could kiss this girl forever.

When she's ready, I push inside. Fuck, being sheathed in her warmth is the best feeling in the world. I close my eyes, and it's like I'm eighteen again, meeting her for the first time.

This. Her. Me.

It's inevitable.

She can't keep denying it. I see it in her eyes. She feels this, too.

"Fuck, Bertie." I grip her throat lightly with one hand. "You feel so good. This pussy was made for me. You hear me? It's mine. You're mine."

Back arching, she whimpers. "Kiss me. Please."

Please?

Who am I to deny my girl what she wants?

Our bodies move as one, every moment effortless. Fuck, why have I been so adamant about not having sex with her? If I'd given in sooner, we'd have been doing this for weeks. God, I'm an idiot.

"Luke." She reaches between us, holding on to the silver chain around my neck.

I want to record the way she says my name and play it over and over again.

"Harder," she pleads. "Fuck me harder, please."

I kiss her neck, whispering against her skin. "If I do, this won't last long."

"I don't care," she cries. "We can do it again."

I bite my lip to keep a laugh from escaping. "Needy, huh?"

She rolls her hips. "I've been dreaming of your cock."

Fuck. This girl and her mouth are going to be the end of me.

"And when you dream of my cock, I'm fucking you hard?"

"I want it to hurt tomorrow," she cries. "I want to know you've been inside me every time I move."

"*Jesus Christ.*"

Challenge accepted.

I let loose everything I've been holding back because I wanted to take my time, relish every second. But she's literally begging, and I can't deny her what she wants.

When Bertie throws her head back and screams, I'm thankful as fuck my mom is working.

The woman beneath me is fucking gorgeous.

Perfect tits and hips and ass and everything.

Her blond hair splays over my pillow like it belongs there.

I'm lost in her.

She has no idea how thoroughly I'm wrapped around her finger.

As she shatters around me, I vow to make her do it again and again. As many times as she'll let me.

"Luke." She grips my biceps. "You feel so good."

Fuck, it's probably the best compliment I've ever gotten.

"I was fucking made for you." I roll my hips, keeping my rhythm steady. "You realize that?"

"Yes," she pants. "Oh, God. Yes."

She squeezes her eyes shut, and fuck if she doesn't orgasm again.

When she opens her eyes this time, they've gone soft. Vulnerable.

I kiss her. Long, slow, intimate. I can't get enough of the taste of her. "I've got you," I whisper between kisses. "I'm going to take such good care of you, baby."

"Mhm." She scratches her nails against my back, marking me.

Sitting back on my heels, I push her legs up until her knees practically kiss her breasts. "Look at you," I croon, diving back in to smatter kisses over her chest. "So flexible. So open for me."

I thrust again and again, and when her eyes roll back, I gently grasp her cheeks. "Open those eyes for me, baby. Let me see you. I want to see you when you come again, got it?"

"I c-can't," she pants. "T-Too—it's too much."

Hit with a wave of determination, I smirk. I can get her there. With the way she responds to my touch? I have no doubt.

Besides, she did tell me that she wants to be sore tomorrow.

When she shatters around me again, I fall with her this time. As I slow my strokes, I bear more of my weight against her, but not all of it. I need to be closer. Skin to skin. We're both damp with sweat, but I don't care. It's a sign of a job well done.

Smoothing her hair off her forehead, I take her in. Blue eyes and pale skin with just a few tiny freckles on her nose. She's so fucking beautiful.

She cups my jaw, rubbing her thumb over my bottom lip. I can't help but wonder if she's studying me, memorizing me, the way I am her.

I don't want to let her go, but I need to get rid of the condom.

I allow myself another minute before I slip out from between her legs and get up.

"Stay there." I put up a firm hand as I back away. "I'll be right back."

Since we're alone in the house, I cross the hall into the bathroom naked and wrap the condom in toilet paper and throw it away. I wash my hands, then wet a washcloth with warm water.

When I return, Bertie is exactly where I left her, but as I drink her in, she covers her breasts with her arm.

I pull it away. "Don't get shy on me now. Let me see you."

Her cheeks pinken, but she doesn't put her arm back. Her eyes instead drop to my dick.

"I thought you came."

"I did."

I press the warm cloth gently to her pussy, hating the way she flinches slightly. I should've been gentler, but I wanted to give her what she asked for.

"You're hard again already?" Her tone is high-pitched, like the idea that I could still be turned on is preposterous.

"My dream girl is naked in my bed, and you think I'm not going to be permanently hard?"

She frowns, her body deflating. "I'm not your dream girl."

I meet her gaze, licking my lips. "You are."

"But I'm…"

"Perfect," I finish for her. "To me, you're perfect."

I toss the cloth into my hamper and lie beside her, gathering her body close so we're facing each other. She hooks her leg around me, and it's a dangerous temptation, having her pussy this close to my dick again.

"I swear I didn't come here for this."

I play with a strand of her hair. Wrapping it around my finger. "I know."

With a hand on my chest, she caresses my skin. "I still don't … I don't know if I'm ready for something serious. The whole boyfriend and girlfriend title thing. But I…"

My heart leaps with hope.

"Maybe we could try dating?" she suggests, her brows furrowed. "See where this thing goes?"

I nod eagerly, perhaps too eagerly, with the way her smile grows.

I'd call her my girlfriend now if she'd let me, but I can be patient. Tommy might be a douche, but she obviously had feelings for him for a long time.

I just hope she can have feelings for me, too.

"Yeah, B. Let's do that."

She kisses my cheek and snuggles into me.

I can't say I've got the girl yet, but I'm one step closer.

NINE

Bertie
9 weeks later

I BURST INSIDE MY DORM WITH THE PLASTIC pharmacy bag crinkled in my grip. I chugged two bottles of water on the way back from the store, and my bladder is ready to burst.

Dumping the contents out of the bag onto the couch, I sort through the various boxes. I got all kinds of tests. Strip tests. Plus and minus. Pregnant or Not Pregnant.

It's a bit excessive, but I wasn't sure which would be

best. I've never taken one before, and I shouldn't have to now. Since the day I stopped by Luke's to give him his gift and we ended up in bed, we haven't had sex again. And even that day, we were careful. I always take my birth control, and he used a condom.

Though I wouldn't have minded making it a regular thing, he's been insistent that we take it slow and not make whatever is growing between us about sex.

Growing between us—like a child growing inside me.

Bile rises in my throat, which only makes my panic spiral more pronounced.

Pregnancy equals vomiting, so am I feeling sick because of my racing thoughts or because there's a tiny human inside me?

I'm not opposed to kids, but I'm still in college. I thought I'd be at least thirty before I had my first.

I scoop up the box containing the test that will read either Pregnant or Not Pregnant and lock myself in the bathroom. The lock isn't necessary, since I live alone now, but it makes me feel a little better.

My cycles have always been consistent, especially on birth control, but I've been so busy with my last semester of college that I didn't even think about it being late until I was digging in the bathroom cabinet for my hairspray and spotted an unopened box of tampons.

Breaths coming quickly, I scan through the directions

and do my business. Then I dip the stick, recap it, and wait.

Within seconds, the walls of the bathroom close in on me, so I stride out and pace my dorm room.

There's no way I'm pregnant. We only had sex *one* time. Something's just up with my body, and my period is a little late.

A little late? More like a lot late.

I can't have a baby.

I'm not ready to be a mom.

I don't even know *how* to be a mom. My mother clearly hasn't modeled any good parental skills for me.

I want to be a mom—a good one—but not now. Not yet. I've barely figured out my life. I don't even have a job lined up.

There is my inheritance, but chances are, if I am pregnant, my parents will figure out a way to snatch that from me. They can be petty.

I take a deep breath and check the time.

My fate should be decided at this point.

Once I'm inside the bathroom, I close my eyes and count to ten.

Those ten seconds are all that separate the Bertie of before with the new Bertie. The Bertie who looks at the test that very clearly says **Pregnant.**

My head swims, and I quickly stumble my way to the couch, fearful I might pass out.

Pregnant.

There's ... there's a baby inside me.

I don't have the mental capacity to cope with this.

There's no stopping the tears that spring to my eyes and course down my cheeks.

What am I going to do?

How am I going to tell Luke?

A fear that I've never felt before settles heavily in my stomach. Not a fear of telling him—knowing Luke, he'll take it in stride like he does everything else, but a fear of the unknown.

I don't have any experience with kids—nothing to gauge how I might handle taking care of a child.

Another thought sinks into my brain, this one coming to me more slowly. I *don't* have to go through with this.

But almost as soon as I have the thought, I dismiss it.

This might not be planned, but I ... I *want* this baby.

Am I scared? Absolutely.

Terrified would be more fitting.

This wasn't the plan, but plans change for a reason.

I press my hand to my stomach.

A baby. My baby. Luke's baby.

I see it then, when I close my eyes. The future. Holding an infant in my arms in the hospital. Cheering a child on when they say their first word and take their first step. First days of school and bike rides and days at the beach. Birthdays and scraped knees and soft kisses to their head.

My fear isn't gone, and there's a good chance my emotions will never recover, but I'll be okay.

We'll be okay.

But what if the test is wrong?

Panic swamps me all over again.

Stupidly, I dumped out the little cup I peed in, so if I want to take another test, I'll have to start again.

Standing, I smooth my shirt, then I shuffle to the table and scoop up the whole assortment of tests and head back to the bathroom.

I need to be sure before I...

A. Continue to freak out.

B. Plan out a child's whole future, only to find out that, *oops*, the test was faulty and I'm not pregnant.

C. Tell Luke I'm pregnant and then have to tell him *oops false alarm*.

D. All of the above.

While I wait to look at the handful of tests I've taken, I do a quick Google search. Within three minutes, I know. Not only is every test positive, but the internet has made it clear that false negatives are far more likely than false positives.

It's true, then.

I'm pregnant.

Fuck.

The extra tests were supposed to make me feel better, but here I am, bursting into tears again.

I cover my face with my hands.

It's going to be okay.

But today, I'm allowed to freak out and sink into my feelings.

Tomorrow, I'll feel better.

Tomorrow, it'll be okay.

TOMORROW ISN'T BETTER.

Neither is the next day.

I freak out about the what-ifs.

What if I hurt the baby when I drank a few weekends ago?

Is Advil harmful to fetuses? Have I taken any recently?

What if I'm not a good mom?

It's not until I go to the doctor with my best friend Rosie by my side that I begin to feel better.

Baby is safe. Baby is good. Baby is healthy.

I can do this.

Hopefully *we* can do this.

I just have to tell Luke…

For what comes next, read Bertie and Luke's full-length novel (and the final book in The Boys series) Honest Boys Don't Play, coming 2025.

www.ingramcontent.com/pod-product-compliance
Lightning Source LLC
LaVergne TN
LVHW031613060526
838201LV00065B/4828